Tod and the
Sand Pirates

by

Anthony Masters

Illustrated by Harriet Buckley

You do not need to read this page – just get on with the book!

Published in 2004 in Great Britain by
Barrington Stoke Ltd, Sandeman House, Trunk's Close
55 High Street, Edinburgh EH1 1SR

This edition based on *Tod and the Sand Pirates*, published
by Barrington Stoke in 2003

ISBN 1-842991-55-8

Printed by Polestar Wheatons Ltd

Meet The Author – Anthony Masters

What is your favourite animal?
My bantams
What is your favourite boy's name?
David
What is your favourite girl's name?
Penny
What is your favourite food?
Chinese food
What is your favourite music?
Mexican
What is your favourite hobby?
Canoeing

Meet The Illustrator – Harriet Buckley

What is your favourite animal?
A cat
What is your favourite boy's name?
Ernest
What is your favourite girl's name?
Emily
What is your favourite food?
Spinach
What is your favourite music?
"There She Goes" by The Las
What is your favourite hobby?
Playing the harmonica

For Samuel James Anthony Kammin
a beloved grandson
with special love

Contents

Chapter 1

WOLF

Tod and Billy sped along the beach on their sand buggies. The wind filled the red sails.

Then, all at once, the wind changed. Billy's buggy was blown over and his mast broke.

Billy fell out and banged his arm on a rock. Tod turned his buggy into the wind and stopped. The red sails of his buggy flapped.

Tod got out and ran over to Billy. "Are you OK?"

"I think so." Billy got slowly to his feet and looked down at his smashed buggy. "I was never any good with these things." He rubbed his sore arm. "What are we going to do?"

That will take days to fix

"Get on my buggy," said Tod. "There's room for two."

Then they heard the wail of a fog horn.

"It's the sand pirates!" Billy was scared. "Now we're in a real mess."

"We can sail faster than them," said Tod. "Don't be scared."

There had been no rain for months. The rivers had dried up and the sea had shrunk back. Fresh water was hard to find. Tod's parents had gone to look for some in the far west. They wouldn't be back for days.

Tod and his friend Billy, who was an ex-Biker, were going up north. They had been told they could find fresh water there.

It was not just water that was hard to find. There was no fuel. No-one could go anywhere. The gangs of Bikers had no

3

petrol to put in the tanks of their motorbikes.

Now Tod and Billy could see the sand pirates' huge ship. Her rusty wheels clanked and her fog horn wailed.

They could see the name on her side. WOLF.

"Let's get away fast," said Tod.

They ran back to Tod's sand buggy. Tod turned the buggy round so its sails filled with wind again.

They took off fast, going north again. But WOLF had huge sails and went even faster.

"They're getting closer," Billy said. Now they could see WOLF's flag with the skull and crossbones on it.

Then the wind dropped.

Tod and Billy's sand buggy came to a stop.

So did WOLF.

But soon WOLF began to move off again.

"There's no wind," said Tod. "Why aren't they stuck like us?"

"They're using pedal power," said Billy. "They must have lots of slaves working the pedals below the decks. They'll easily catch up with us now."

WOLF came nearer and nearer. She was very large, almost as big as a house.

"We can't just sit here," said Billy.

"Pray for wind. That's all we can do."

As she came closer, Tod could see that there were a lot of pirates standing on her deck.

"They've got laser swords," he yelled. "Don't try to run for it. Just keep still. Those swords can kill from 100 metres away."

"WOLF's closer than 100 metres," Billy said. He put his hands up in surrender.

So did Tod.

Chapter 2
Pirates

As WOLF came closer, Tod and Billy saw that a wooden platform was being pushed out from the deck.

There was a young woman in a safety harness tied to the platform. She wore a sand suit and a helmet. In her hand she held a laser sword.

The blade of the sword flashed. The laser beam hit the mast of Tod's sand buggy.

"That was close," said Tod.

"Too close," replied Billy.

Now the platform was just above them.

"Surrender!" the young woman shouted at them.

"We *have* surrendered," Billy's voice shook.

"We're going to Paradise Island. We hear there's fresh water there," she told them.

"Is there?" asked Tod, as if he didn't know.

"What do you know about Paradise Island?" the young woman asked.

"Nothing at all," Billy yelled up at her.

"Paradise Island belongs to Maxted, the rock star, and his girlfriend Scarlet," said the young woman. "But if there *is* fresh water there we'll soon take it over."

"What's your name?" asked Tod.

"Captain Silver," she told him. "You're our prisoners now. We're going to take you on board WOLF."

A wooden cage came slowly down from WOLF. On top of the cage stood two huge men with tattoos.

"I know them," said Billy. "They used to be Bikers like me."

"Put up your hands and get into the cage," Captain Silver told Tod and Billy.

"But what about my sand buggy?" asked Tod. "I don't want to lose it."

"It's no use to you now," Captain Silver told him.

She watched the two boys get out of the buggy and walk over to the cage.

Tod looked back sadly at his buggy. Captain Silver pointed her laser sword at him.

"Get into that cage," she said. "And hurry up."

"Do what she says," begged Billy.

"I'm doing what she says," replied Tod. "Just for now, anyway."

The cage was lifted up onto WOLF. Then Tod and Billy were left waiting in the cage for over half an hour.

"What are they going to do to us?" Billy kept asking.

"It would be awful if they made us into their slaves," said Tod. "But don't forget WOLF's going the way we want to go. She's helping us get up north."

"But Silver said that when she gets to Paradise Island the pirates will take over the water. Maxted and Scarlet don't have an army and can't stop her." Billy was very scared now.

"I know all that," said Tod. "But we're still a long way from Paradise Island. Before we get there I'll try to destroy this ship."

"How?"

"We could get the slaves on our side against Captain Silver."

"You always think big, don't you?" said Billy.

Slowly the wind got up again. WOLF's sails began to fill.

"We'll soon be on our way," Captain Silver told everyone. "Get to your places now."

Sand was blowing around everywhere. Tod and Billy pulled on their masks to protect their faces. They did not want to choke.

"If we can escape from WOLF, I'll get Maxted and Scarlet to pipe some of their water from Paradise Island to the mainland," said Tod.

"If we try to escape, Captain Silver may tie us to the mast and take away our masks. Then the sand will choke us and we'll die before we get to Paradise Island," said Billy.

Soon after that, Captain Silver came to the door of the cage. She had some ex-Bikers with her. They had skull and crossbone tattoos on their faces, and huge, strong arms.

"So *you're* Tod." Captain Silver pushed her laser sword through the wooden bars of the cage. "I've heard a lot about you."

"Nothing bad, I hope," said Tod.

"You're both going to die," said Silver, with a grin. "It'll teach the other slaves to behave. I'm going to keel haul you."

"What's that?" asked Billy.

"Ropes will drag you under the ship," Silver told him. "You'll die in agony." Then she left them.

"Do you think she's really going to kill us?" asked Billy.

"Not if you do what I tell you," snapped Tod. "Silver's done something stupid. Look over here. Her laser sword has burnt away part of the cage." Tod showed him where a wooden bar had been burnt black.

Tod made sure no-one was looking. Then he hit at the wooden bar with his fist – and it broke away.

"We can just get through the gap," he told Billy.

When they were out of the cage, Tod and Billy ran to a pile of crates and hid behind them.

"We'll jump on the next pirates we see and grab their sand suits," said Tod.

Billy and Tod hid behind the crates and waited.

After a long time, two young pirates walked along the deck and came up to the crates.

"I'd do anything for a drink of fresh water," said one of the pirates. "Do you think …?"

Before the pirate could finish his sentence, Tod hit him hard. Billy did the same to the other pirate. They fell to the ground.

Tod and Billy put on the pirates' sand suits. Then they tied them up, back to back, with some cord that Billy had found amongst the crates. They dragged the two pirates back to the cage.

"They'll soon be found," said Tod. "So we don't have much time."

Chapter 3
The Reef

No-one even looked at Tod and Billy as they crossed the deck in their pirate sand suits. Everyone was too busy catching the wind in WOLF's sails.

Then, a pirate was blown over WOLF's side. His ropes broke free and his sails flapped.

He rolled over and over on the dry sand. When he came to a stop he was just a ball of sand.

"Grab that pirate's ropes," hissed Tod. "If we can work on his sail, no-one will spot us."

But working on the sail was very hard. It was huge, and when it filled with wind Tod and Billy were almost dragged off their feet.

"I can't hold on," yelled Billy.

"Yes, you can," Tod told him. "If you go over WOLF's side you'll end up as a sand ball, just like that pirate back there."

The wind was now driving WOLF along at great speed. Then Billy saw a huge line of rock ahead.

"It's a reef!" he yelled. "We're going to crash!"

Tod gazed ahead in horror. The reef looked like a mountain. The smell of rotting weed and dead fish hit them as they came nearer.

"Stop the ship!" yelled Captain Silver.

Slowly WOLF began to turn and at last came to a halt.

"Get the sails down," Silver yelled. Tod looked round at the rest of the crew to see how to do this.

Tod and Billy worked fast. At last they got their sail down and rolled it up.

"Stay calm. Don't panic, Billy," said Tod.

It's easy to say that, thought Billy, as Silver came up on deck with her Bikers.

"Let out the slaves," she ordered. "Let out the slaves now."

The pirate crew opened some hatches. Out of them came the slaves. They wore old tops and faded jeans. Their bare feet were bleeding.

Tod saw that the slaves' tops were torn at the back. Their skin was cut and raw.

They must have been beaten to make them work harder, thought Tod.

"We'll have to drag the ship over the reef," said Captain Silver. "The slaves can't do it alone. Everyone will have to help – even Tod and Billy."

Now we'll be found out, thought Tod. But no-one had time to check on the cage. Everyone was busy getting out the ropes.

The huge, dark green reef rose up above them.

Chapter 4
Dragging WOLF

It was very hard work dragging WOLF up the reef. Tod and Billy had never felt so worn out.

They were close to the top of the reef when Captain Silver and her Bikers came up on deck.

"Stop!" she yelled.

It looked as if WOLF might slide back, but the slaves and pirates were just able to hold her in place.

"Don't think you're going to escape," Captain Silver shouted. "You're all going to die in the end."

Then one of the slaves spoke up. "We've all worked hard for you. If you harm any of us, we'll let WOLF slide back."

"How dare you speak to me like that?" Captain Silver was very angry.

But the other slaves began to protest and she changed her mind. "Carry on pulling," she said. "We've got to get WOLF over the reef or we'll all die."

She walked off fast with her huge Bikers.

"Thanks," said Tod to the slave who had spoken up for them all.

"We know you attacked two of the pirates. You're one of us now," the slave told him.

They started to pull WOLF over the reef again. "There's one thing Silver hasn't thought about," the slave said.

"What's that?" asked Billy.

"Octopeds. They're huge squids and they live behind this reef in the next valley. They've learnt to live without water and they're land monsters now."

"Have you been this way before?"

"When I was a free man," said the slave sadly.

"You'll be a free man again," Tod told him, "if you join with us and fight Silver and the pirates."

"We've nothing to fight with," said the slave. "And they've got laser swords."

"Trust us," said Tod. "We'll find a way."

At last WOLF got to the top of the reef. Captain Silver let them rest for a short time.

"Look down in the valley," said the slave. "Silver's going to get a shock."

Tod, Billy and the slave looked down at the valley below. There were weeds everywhere. The light was dim, but they could just see something moving in the weeds.

"We must cross that valley – and get over the next reef." Captain Silver was standing beside them.

She must know we have escaped, thought Tod. *I wonder how?*

Captain Silver stared down at the valley. "What's going on down there?" she asked.

"Octopeds," said Tod. "This slave told me that they were once huge squid, but they've now become land monsters and can live without water."

"What can they do to us?" asked Captain Silver. She was not going to attack Tod and Billy now she knew they were all in danger.

"The Octopeds have deadly stings," said the slave. "Just one of those stings will kill you."

"We'll have to be careful then," said Captain Silver. Then she yelled out her orders. "We'll be clear of the reef by dawn. But you'll need to work harder and faster," she told everyone.

As they came down the reef, it was almost impossible to stop WOLF from crashing down into the valley.

Several times the slaves and pirates slipped and the ship began to slide.

But each time WOLF was just saved from sliding away down the reef.

Captain Silver came back to see how they were getting on.

"We need to be armed," Tod told her. "All your slaves could die from the stings of those Octopeds. Then you would have no-one to work the ship. Let us have some laser swords."

"But then you can attack me," said Captain Silver. She looked angry.

"We won't attack you," Billy told her.

"You have to take that risk," said Tod.

"I'll leave some of my Bikers with you," said Silver. "They can protect you while you get the sand ship through the valley."

She started to yell at everyone. "Can you all hear me? We are going into the valley of the Octopeds. They all have deadly stings. Keep away from them. My Bikers will be there to look after you if there's a crisis."

"What does she mean – *if* there's a crisis?" said Billy. "It's going to be crisis time all the way down that valley."

Chapter 5

The Battle with the Octopeds

At last, after a lot of slipping and sliding, the huge ship got down to the valley.

But it was even harder pulling WOLF along the valley floor and trying to miss the hidden Octopeds.

"How did Silver get to be boss?" asked Billy.

"She's very strong," said the slave. "And she's a terrific fighter."

An Octoped came out of the dark, roaring and barking. It was a scary sight. It had long legs and was six metres high. Its shining eyes stuck out of its head and its long tongue flickered out from its slit of a mouth.

"Be careful of its tongue!" yelled Tod. "I bet you that's where the sting comes from."

Billy let go of his rope and moved away fast. But he was too late.

The Octoped didn't sting Billy, but it wrapped some of its legs around him and dragged him away from the ship.

"Give me that laser sword," Tod yelled at one of the Bikers.

"I won't!" he replied. "Why should I do that?"

"You've been told to look after us," shouted a slave.

Tod jumped on the Biker and hit him hard. The Biker fell onto the sand and dropped his laser sword.

Tod picked it up and pushed on through the weeds.

"Where are you going?" Captain Silver asked. She was standing in front of him, laser sword in hand.

"I'm going to save Billy," Tod said. "And don't try to stop me."

"I'm not going to stop you," said Captain Silver. "I'm coming with you."

"Without your Bikers?" said Tod.

"*I* can beat you any time," she told Tod. "But let's get Billy back first."

Together, Tod and Captain Silver pushed on through the weeds.

Then Tod saw the shining eyes of the Octoped and heard Billy cry out in pain.

"We're coming, Billy!" Tod yelled. "Just hang on."

Tod and Captain Silver rushed at the Octoped, but there were others coming nearer.

"I'll protect you, Tod," said Captain Silver.

"Thanks," yelled Tod. He heard the roars of the Octopeds as Captain Silver began to zap them with her laser.

The Octoped that had Billy shot out its tongue and just missed Tod, who hit back with the blade of his laser sword.

The Octoped gave a wild cry and dropped Billy.

"Are you OK?" asked Tod.

"I think so," said Billy, trying to stand up.

"Let's get back to the ship," yelled Captain Silver. "You've got a lot more work to do there."

"Thanks," said Tod.

"You and I could have a fight," said Captain Silver. "Then we'll see which of us gets killed."

"Any time," said Tod.

"Are you mad?" hissed Billy.

"That's a date then," said Captain Silver.

Tod hoped it was a date she would forget.

By the next morning, WOLF had been dragged over the last ridge of the next reef and down onto the sand on the other side.

"Get back below deck," yelled Captain Silver at the slaves. "And start using the pedals."

Everyone got back on board WOLF. The slaves opened the hatches and went below. They began to pedal.

Tod and Billy were just planning what to do next when Captain Silver came up.

"I see you've still got your laser sword. But if you want to keep it you'll have to kill me first." She moved to an open part of the deck and waited for Tod.

"Don't fight her," said Billy. "You'll lose."

"I've got to fight her," said Tod.
He walked over to Captain Silver. She had
her laser sword in her hand.

But just as Tod and Captain Silver were
about to start their fight, Billy saw a hot
air balloon flying towards WOLF.

"The wind's got up again," he yelled.
"And there's a balloon coming over—"

Captain Silver looked up. So did Tod.
"We'll have our fight later," she said and
gave some orders to her Bikers.

They opened the hatches again and the
slaves came up to help the crew with the
ropes that held the sails. There was a great
flapping sound as they began to fill with
wind.

The hot air balloon was about to land on
the open part of the deck where Tod and

Captain Silver had been going to have their fight.

"No!" yelled Tod. "Take off again."

But the people in the balloon landed on the deck. Billy saw it was the rock star Maxted and his girlfriend Scarlet.

It's no good being rich, thought Billy, *if you have nothing to spend your money on.*

"We come in peace," said Maxted.

"Don't you understand? You've landed on a pirate ship," Tod told them.

"We want to share our water with everyone," said Maxted.

How stupid can you get? thought Billy. *Captain Silver and her pirates won't share the water with anyone.*

"Tie Maxted and Scarlet to the mast," yelled Captain Silver. "And Tod and Billy too."

Chapter 6
Strapped to the Mast

Maxted, Scarlet, Billy and Tod were tied to the masts of the ship. The balloon lay on the deck.

Then WOLF sped off on its way to Paradise Island.

Billy knew they were all going to die.

Soon they could see Paradise Island sticking out of the sand. Tod could just see a glint of water.

"Landing on this ship was a really stupid thing to do," Tod yelled at Maxted.

"We came in peace," Maxted replied.

"This is a pirate ship."

"We were visiting everyone who's still alive," said Maxted. "We want to pipe water from Paradise Island to the mainland so that everyone can have some. It's the only way we can stop all this fighting. We must share."

"You haven't got anything *to* share now you're strapped to a mast," Tod told him.

"There's one of those hot winds coming," yelled Billy. "A real scorcher. Can't you get Captain Silver to rescue us again, Tod?"

"She only came to the rescue last time because she enjoys a good fight," said Tod.

"Then we've had it," said Billy. "The scorcher will fry us to a crisp."

Then WOLF came to a sudden stop. Her limp sails started to flap.

"We're sinking!" shouted Scarlet in horror.

Slowly the sand began to creep over the decks.

"We *are* sinking," yelled Billy.

"It's quicksand!" shouted Tod.

WOLF sank deeper and deeper into the quicksand. Everyone was very scared.

Tod tried to break the cords that tied his arms and legs to the mast. But they held

firm. Then he saw Captain Silver below him.

"I'm going to cut your ropes," she said.

"What – with a laser sword?" yelled Billy. "You'll fry us faster than the scorcher."

But Captain Silver only smiled. "Hold onto the mast – and watch this."

She zapped at Tod, Billy, Maxted and Scarlet with her laser sword – and all four did a quick turn, grabbed the mast and slid down.

Once on the deck Tod hissed at the other three. "Now – while she's telling the crew what to do – we'll get to the balloon."

Captain Silver yelled at the crew. "Do NOT leave the ship. I repeat – do NOT leave the ship."

As she went on giving orders, Tod, Billy, Maxted and Scarlet ran to the hot air balloon and jumped into the basket.

"We're off!" said Maxted as he pulled up the anchor.

"What about the slaves?" asked Tod. "We must try and save them."

"I think they can look after themselves," said Scarlet. Tod saw the slaves rush for the lifeboats – which were small sand ships. They were so light that they did not sink into the quicksand.

"What about Captain Silver?" asked Tod. "After all, she saved our lives."

"Don't worry. One of the pirates is getting her into a lifeboat," said Billy.

As the hot air balloon left the sinking ship and flew off to Paradise Island, Maxted said, "I was a fool to trust Captain Silver."

"He trusts everyone," Scarlet told them.

"That's a terrible risk," Billy warned them.

"We'll work out a plan to pipe water from Paradise Island to the mainland," said Tod. "Everyone can have some if they obey the new water laws."

"What new water laws?" asked Billy.

"The laws we're going to make," said Tod. He gazed out over the miles of dry sand. This was now the only world they knew.

Who is Barrington Stoke?

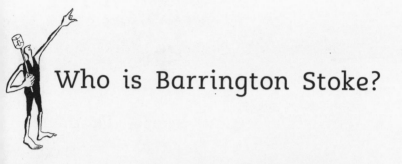

Barrington Stoke went from place to place with his lamp in his hand. Everywhere he went, he told stories to children. Some were happy, some were sad, some were funny and some were scary.

The children always wanted more. When it got dark, they had to go home to bed. They went to look for Barrington Stoke the next day, but he had gone.

The children never forgot the stories. They told them to each other and to their children and their grandchildren. You see, good stories are magic and they can live for ever.

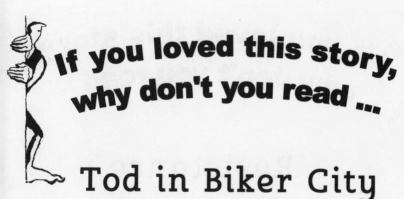

Tod in Biker City

by Anthony Masters

Could you survive in a world that had become a total desert? Tod's father finds a source of water but his discovery puts the whole family in great danger. It's up to Tod to save them!

4u2read.ok!

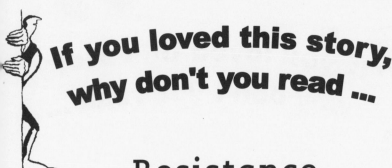

If you loved this story, why don't you read ...

Resistance

by Ann Jungman

Do you ever disagree with your parents? Jan is ashamed when his Dutch father sides with the Germans during the Second World War. Only Elli is his friend. Can Jan find a way to help the Resistance?

4u2read.ok!